FOUND *by the* LONER

HALLIE BENNETT

BOOKS BY THIS AUTHOR

CHAPTER ONE

NORA

"I'll be fine. I'll be fine." The repetitive chant floats in the air as my booted feet track through a landscape of falling snow. Earlier, the forecast had predicted an inch or two of fluffy white flakes, which to my mind meant trekking up Black Mountain for a magical winter photoshoot—the kind I've dreamed about creating since moving to the small mountain town of High Ridge three months ago.

As a Southern woman, the experience of snow thrills and terrifies me, but letting fear stop me from doing what I want is a thing of the past... most of the time. Some days are easier than others, but after a couple of years working with a therapist, I've learned how to work through my fear instead of allowing it to control my actions.

A dose of fear can be healthy, though. Stop you from making dangerous decisions.

The errant thought pushes through my litany of reassurances. "I'll be fine. I'm okay. It's just a bit of snow." *More than a bit.*

Icy air swirls around my bare legs as I continue forward, determined not to turn back until I get what I've come for—the perfect snowy shot. It's what my followers expect after how much

I've hyped this dream shoot anytime the weatherman predicts wintry flakes.

Growing up, I never would have imagined taking as many pictures of myself as I have, and I definitely never would've shared them for the world to see and judge. Part of my issues with fear stemmed from being bullied for my weight at school and home; my perfect Southern belle of a mother scolded and insulted me for years.

It wasn't until I turned twenty-five that I decided that enough was enough.

Miserable and alone, I started therapy, which led to considerable changes in my life, like quitting my dead-end job to become a body-positive social media influencer. At first, the pictures I posted were only meant as a personal victory, but within weeks, the account blew up.

Millions of people messaged me encouragement and shared their own body-positive journeys, full of struggle like mine. Now, my full-time career is finding products that work for a non-traditional body type and producing high-quality photos known for their ethereal aesthetic, proving how curvy girls are beautiful, too.

Which is why I find myself on a wild mission up the mountain in freezing temperatures.

Dangerous temperatures.

Shaking off the persistent worry niggling at the back of my mind, I keep walking for another fifteen minutes when a vision of white-dusted evergreens behind a boulder elicits a smile of glee.

This is it.

Whipping off my backpack and coat, a shiver wracks my thinly gowned body—the sheer chiffon gorgeous but not practical for the weather—and I hurry to remove my snow-covered boots. Thank goodness no one's around to see how ridiculous I must look, but it won't take long to get the shots I need.

Setting up my camera equipment in the deepening snow, I chance a live video for my followers. "Hey, guys! I'm out on Black Mountain today for my Fairy in an Enchanted Forest shoot. As you know, I've been waiting to do this one while it snows, and today I got my wish!" Panning around the small clearing, giant flakes flutter to the ground. "I'll tag the gown and gold makeup I'm wearing later because it's freezing at the moment. But anything for the shot, right?"

After a flirtatious wink, I end the video to climb onto the boulder like it's something I've done a million times before. *Not.* Bare feet slide on the slick stone, and the warnings in my head get louder.

Turn back now.

In another five minutes. You've got this.

"No big deal, just a few quick shots..." I mutter, situating myself towards the camera, a tiny remote for the timer clenched in my fist. The high slit of the dress drifts open to expose one gold-dusted thigh, and another shiver works its way through my limbs.

Fuck, it's cold.

Pressing a button on the timer, I get down to business—arching my back one way, tilting my head another, adding subtle changes to my expression—until an ominous cracking shrieks from above.

Winter birds scatter from the treetops as a large bough breaks from one tree, heading on a collision course for me.

"Shit!" Scrambling to avoid impalement, the timer falls from my hand, and I unthinkingly stretch to save it, setting off a series of terrible events. The quick movement sends my body skittering off the slick stone to tumble back down the mountain in a bone-crushing dive.

A brief scream of terror echoes in the forest before I slam to a stop, and everything goes black.

CHAPTER TWO

RHETT

My German Shepherd, Tully, runs ahead in the wintry forest as we walk our usual path around the property. Massive snowflakes fall gently to the ground like they've been doing for the past three hours, and the peaceful atmosphere soothes my soul after a week full of work and social commitments. I prefer sticking to my own company the majority of the time—the exceptions being Micah and Asa's families.

It still amazes me that my younger brother and best friend managed to find women in such quick succession of each other. Hell, Micah's having a baby soon! Yet, my only companion is Tully.

Which didn't used to bother you so much.

Guess being surrounded by loving couples will do that to a man—remind him of what he doesn't have.

"Tully, come on, boy! It's time we head home." The arctic temperature is beginning to seep through my layers of wool and flannel, and I'm ready to relax in front of the fire at home. However, my damn dog seems to have other ideas as he continues to race forward, his incessant barking disrupting the previous calm.

He's probably tracked down a rabbit or some other poor creature, but I'm not in the mood to indulge his hunting instincts.

"Leave it, Tully. I'm cold and—" My words and footsteps stutter to a halt as I find the focus of his attention. A woman lies in the snow, melting crystals of white glistening on her exposed skin. Glancing between my dog and the woman, I wonder if I'm hallucinating.

Dressed in a golden confection of chiffon and lace, she looks like a fucking angel.

An unprotected angel who'll freeze to death from hypothermia if I don't get her somewhere safe and warm.

Instinct leaps to the forefront as I jog to help. Trembling fingers unzip my jacket before draping it over her prone body, grateful to see the steady rise and fall of her chest. I work my arms under her knees and back before cradling her against my chest—a precious feminine bundle now under my protection.

The smooth skin of her cheeks shimmers in the sunlight.

She's fucking glowing.

And I'm reminded of Asa and his woman, Poppy.

He found her stranded on the side of the road and kept her. Maybe the mountain has gifted me in the same way? Dropping this divine bounty of curves and silk straight into my lap?

Get real, motherfucker. The mountain hasn't gifted you shit.

Everyone in High Ridge knows my younger brother Micah is the lucky charmer of the family. I'm just the poor bastard who's tried to keep him in line until his wife Kate came along, and now, with Asa tamed by his wife Poppy, I'm the sole grumpy loner on the mountain.

No way fate's going to reward me with a fallen angel.

Sufficiently reminded that I don't live in a fucking fairy tale, I begin the journey home—my priority to warm her up and make sure she isn't otherwise injured. There hadn't been a stain of blood beneath her, but something must've happened for her to end up unconscious during the flurries of a snowstorm.

Or to explain where the rest of her winter gear is...

Tully traipses beside us, glancing upward every now and again to check on his ward, a pitiful mewl whining in his throat. "It's alright, boy. We'll get her home and safe soon. You did a good job finding her," I praise, refusing to imagine what would've happened if we hadn't gone on a walk today. Tightening my grip, I cuddle the woman closer, the coolness of her nose and cheeks burrowing into my neck.

Won't be long now, angel.

Stomping the packed snow off my boots in my cabin's mudroom, I stride down the hall to the master suite before depositing her on the king-sized mattress. Translucent layers of chiffon spill over the navy comforter. Fiery red hair forms a halo of light amid the sea of dark blue beneath her. And all I can do is stare in awe.

She's the most perfect thing I've ever seen, and she's lying in my bed.

Smoothing a fingertip over the back of her hand, a spark burns its way to my heart. Not a dream, then. A part of me still wondered, but no, she's a living, breathing angel.

And it's my job to make sure she stays that way.

CHAPTER THREE

NORA

"*H*ey, *butter ball over here!" Laughter follows as I hurry past the popular kids' lunch table, where two guys wave me closer while a group of girls giggle.*

Ignore them and they'll leave you alone.

Taking a seat at an empty table, I keep my head down, focusing on eating calmly, making every bite last so I'm not left sitting alone doing nothing. At least if I'm eating, I can pretend it's not pathetic to sit by myself. My mind can focus on the crispy breading of the chicken sandwich or the salty crinkle fries instead of the taunting across the cafeteria.

"Come on angel girl. Another sip, that's it. Good girl." Warm praise interrupts the memory, seeping underneath a fuzzy layer of disorientation, as liquid heat slides down my throat. I fight to the surface of consciousness—to learn who owns the low, gravelly voice urging me to drink more—but the past claims me again as I slip back into a restless sleep.

"You can't wear that." My mother points in disgust at the sleeveless dress skimming my curves. "No one wants to see flabby arms, especially at your cousin's wedding. Cover up, so we can leave. You've already made us late."

The confidence I'd felt moments before evaporates, and I head back to my room for a cardigan, careful to keep my steps light so another comment about 'sounding like a stomping elephant' isn't forthcoming. Tears blur the rainbow of colors in my closet until I quickly blink them away. Now's not the time for crying.

Besides, I'm sure something else will happen today to remind me how unattractive I am, how much of a disappointment...

Tingling awareness arcs over my skin.

Tiny pinpricks of pain.

Gentle warmth driving out the bitter trail of memories.

"Come on, angel." A deep voice reaches through the scattered sensations, but my body resists the insistent call. "Time to wake up, and let me see those pretty eyes." Another wash of heat bleeds into my skin as a dry cloth presses into my neck and chest.

Where am I?

It's uncomfortable to wiggle my toes and fingers, and something heavy lines the length of my body. The stranger continues speaking in a calm, beseeching tone—the timbre's soothing but unfamiliar.

What happened?

Anxiety spikes in my veins—heart roaring to a breakneck pace, threatening to explode—as jumbled images crowd into consciousness. A falling branch. Tumbling down the mountain. A crash into darkness. The moments before my fall replay in vivid color, and I curse my stupidity, moaning in shame and discomfort.

Like one of those book heroines deemed TSTL or too stupid to live, I drove to a mountain during a snowstorm for a couple of photos and ended up unconscious in a stranger's bed, dreaming of bullying from my past.

Nothing like a strong knock to the head to send you straight back to high school, apparently.

Blinking bleary eyes open, the first thing I notice is the man's green gaze—dark like the forest and just as mysterious. The next is a wet lick on the back of my hand, and when I gingerly turn my head, a German Shepherd sits with its head resting on the side of the bed, watching me with concern.

Surrounded by cuties. Not the worst way to wake up.

"You're awake. Finally," the man rumbles, drawing my attention back to him. "How are you feeling?"

"Like I rolled down a mountain during a blizzard," I quip, trying to sit up. How did I land here with a hot mountain man performing first aid on my hypothermic ass?

"Easy, let me help you." Brawny arms curve around my back to help me adjust, and I admire his strength—realizing exactly *how* he was able to carry my unconscious size twenty-four butt to this bed. And the feat makes me regret being knocked out for most of it; I would've enjoyed being held in his arms.

The faint earthy scent of leather and pine tickles my nose, an alluring invitation to snuggle closer and breathe deeply; my head is halfway buried in his neck before I jerk away in embarrassment.

Get it together, Nora.

Those dreams must've done a real number on me, despite all the therapy I've done to recover. Because, deep inside, that girl who longed to be rescued by someone who'd care and protect her is gasping in delight at this new turn of events.

"Thanks... for everything," I murmur, searching my foggy brain for more words. "How'd you find me?"

"You can thank Tully for that." The black and brown shepherd perks up at his name, and a frisson of amusement tugs at my mouth. Guess it was my good luck to have an accident while an adorable rescue dog traipsed the forest. "Mind if I ask what you were doing out there alone without proper winter gear?"

Another burning flush of chagrin rises, and at this point, instead of dying from hypothermia, heatstroke seems a better bet. It's bad enough I tried smelling the man like a damn bloodhound. Now, I have to explain my idiocy over being caught in a snowstorm. After muddling through introductions and the humiliating confession, a hush falls over the room, interrupted only by the pinging of snowflakes against the window.

A nerve tics at the corner of his eye before he growls through clenched teeth. "You endangered yourself over a damn picture? For social media?" He spits out in disgust, and I wince as his opinion of me clearly drops to sub-par levels.

This isn't how rescues happen in the movies. The damsel in distress isn't supposed to fill the knight in shining armor with disdain. There should be lust and fireworks.

Have you ever experienced lust and fireworks?

One of my therapy sessions—an emotional meeting complete with crying—comes to mind. Between scrolling through happy couples on Facebook and enduring another day of no matches on the dating apps, self-pity had ridden me hard, along with self-disgust over my weight.

Memories of how boys used to tease me about my size, insulting me or comparing me to the girl who blew up into a blueberry in Willy Wonka, drowned me in a never-ending deluge of tears. They'd killed my hope that things would be different with men as an adult, and while I appreciated not being called terrible names anymore, blatant disinterest wasn't exactly what I had in mind.

My therapist had listened and let me spill all of my disparaging thoughts like I was lancing a wound, allowing the infected puss to ooze out. With her help that day and many others, I've worked through a lot of my insecurities, but that doesn't mean they've disappeared completely—especially when a man as attractive as Rhett looks at me like I'm used bubblegum stuck to his shoe.

"It wasn't my brightest moment, but I couldn't resist the snow." I glance longingly outside, remembering how happy I'd been hours earlier.

"Angel, it snows nearly every damn week up here. Next time you need to hike through it, let me know; I'll make sure you're staying safe." He waves his phone in the air before tossing it to the nightstand next to the bed. "Especially if your job's expecting such risky behavior."

His offer comes as a surprise until the concern on his face registers. Rhett's not disgusted by me. He's worried—wants to protect me—and the burst of warmth in my chest shoots giddiness through my veins, straight to the teen-aged Nora jumping with glee.

"I'll remember to call you now that we're friends."

"Is that what we are?" I deflate a little at the question, then he continues, "You may regret calling me a friend." He leans back in the chair perched by my side, arms crossing and causing the fabric to pull over taut muscles.

"Why?"

"You haven't been in High Ridge long enough for the gossip to make its rounds, but I'm not exactly a welcome sight in town. Grew up poor in a rundown trailer. Caused lots of trouble with my brother Micah and best friend Asa." He shrugs. "Wouldn't want your reputation to be sullied so quickly by hanging out with me, especially since it sounds like your livelihood depends on social interaction."

"Well, I don't think I have many followers from High Ridge, so we're good on that front." The notion makes me laugh. I definitely don't have a hoard of followers in this small town. No one recognizes me when I shop at the local mom and pop shop; no one ever mentions a favorite shoot of mine at the library. If anyone is a fan, they've kept to themselves, instead of shouting from the rooftops that they live in the same town as me. "Besides, I don't care for bullies, which is what people are if they're punishing you for the past or things out of your control."

Like where you grew up... or your weight.

Rhett remains quiet, dark eyes roving over my face as if deciding whether to believe me or not. Clearing his throat, his chin jerks in a sharp nod of acceptance along with a gruff murmur of gratitude before standing to his feet, and I have to tilt my head back to eye his tall form.

Damn, he's built like a fucking oak tree—solid and very climbable.

"Let's get you into warmer clothes. As pretty as you look, it's time to put on something more practical, angel."

Cool chiffon shifts beneath me, a reminder of the ill-fated photoshoot—glittering gold makeup and all. God, I must look like a mess. *But he called you pretty and an angel!*

Right. Focus on facts, not what my insecurity wants me to believe, I tell myself. Even if Rhett means nothing by them, they're still better than what he could call me.

Like butter ball...

Moving to a wooden chest of drawers, he removes sweatpants, a tee, and a flannel button-down that matches the one he's wearing except it's navy instead of forest green. I imagine him buying a pack of identical flannels—blue, green, red—for ease of access, and it amuses the fashion-lover inside me.

"I'll give you some privacy." The clothes drift to the foot of the bed after he tosses them my way, turning to leave.

"Wait!" Scrambling from the bed, clumsy feet catching on the dress hem, I pitch forward into Rhett's arms.

Sweaty palms brace against his firm chest.

Nails dig into the fabric.

And my treacherous body molds to his.

Breathe.

My lungs fight for a full breath, but they only drag in more of his enticing scent. Sending my hormones careening like the pins at a bowling alley after a lucky strike. Flying every which way in an attempt to lure me closer to the man who's captured their attention.

I'm not sure what possessed me to ask him to stay. Maybe his heroic feat of hauling me through the snow. Maybe the resigned sadness in his voice when he talked about his past. Or maybe I just didn't want to let another opportunity pass me by, didn't want to ignore the spontaneous impulse ensnaring my mind.

Didn't want to lose this miracle fantasy leftover from my lonely years as a teenager.

Hell, if I'm honest, I'm *still* lonely most days—just better at handling it and filling my time and space with positive coping mechanisms.

"I want to thank you properly." The words come out more sultry than I intended, but Rhett's fingers press deeper into my hips, urging me the slightest inch closer, so I don't think he minds. A half-baked plan bounces between my head and my heart—a plan of action and seduction, if I'm brave enough to continue.

"You already have."

"True..." My toes push into the hardwood floor as I lift higher to whisper against his mouth. "But I was thinking of expressing my gratitude in a more tangible way."

Grazing my lips over his in the briefest touch of warning, a spark of electricity leaps between us like a lightning bolt striking the ground, and all hesitancy disappears. Our mouths meet again in a frantic rush, my hands curling into his shirt for balance as his burrow into my fleshy love handles—sure to leave bruises.

The kiss is raw, like bootlegged moonshine and undeniably lethal. Though I started this, Rhett's stealing control. Teeth nipping. Beard scratching. His mouth taking full possession of mine.

Curves melting further into the unyielding masculine form holding me captive, I give him everything he wants—everything he's demanding.

Until he gingerly pushes me away.

No, don't stop.

"We shouldn't be doing this. You're still suffering from exposure; you're not thinking clearly." He shoves his hands in the back pockets of his jeans, forcing the denim tighter against the large erection bulging at the front. My eyes widen, thighs clenching at the irresistible sight.

"I'm afraid we can't blame the weather for my behavior," I tease with a flirtatious smile. "See, I've decided to do what I want these days—fear be damned—because too many years have gone by with me ignoring my wants and needs."

Too many years of bullying from boys at school and my mother to ignore a man who's only been kind, who's obviously as attracted to me as I am to him.

Perhaps too much information for a near stranger, but he needs to understand that I'm perfectly aware of the decisions I'm making.

The muscle along his jaw twitches as he mulls over my words; I didn't think his face could get any more stern, yet the lines of his face tauten like leather being stretched for drying.

"And what, exactly, are you wanting from me?"

A million thoughts clatter in my head, piling on top of each other like the snowflakes outside, until the last one crashes down, obliterating everything else. "Another kiss... and maybe more?" The brazen request feels unreal coming from my mouth. I may be more self-assured after hard work and therapy, but I've never directly propositioned a man.

But how can I resist?

I came out here today to shoot an ethereal photo reminiscent of romantic fairytales, and a knight in shining armor—a fucking prince—literally came to my rescue instead. If that's not the set-up to a sexy, snowed-in situation, I don't know what is!

CHAPTER FOUR

RHETT

How did we end up here?

One moment I'm worried for her health and the next minute I'm devouring her mouth like she's my first gulp of water after an eternity lost in the desert. Surely, that's not what she intended when she offered a kiss of gratitude.

Except it was?

Confusion rattles through my mind, a deadly snake waiting to bite, ensuring I never get too close to figuring out what the hell is going on. Because she can't be serious. It's delusional to believe this angel magically appeared on my mountain, ready to seduce me. The Olson men aren't this lucky. Scratch that, my younger brother Micah is—gaining love and a baby on the way after a one-night stand is irrefutable proof.

"If you're not interested, no hard feelings." Her curious gaze drops to my dick, straining the bounds of my pants. Clearly, she sees exactly how interested I am.

But skipping straight to sex with Nora?

A woman who lay in my bed ice cold after a freak accident not ten minutes ago?

It doesn't feel right.

Everything's moving too fast—from her recovery to my electrified response to her. All of it reeks of Micah, and the comparison doesn't sit well. For years, I've wrangled my younger brother's wild antics, yet here I am considering throwing caution to the wind and indulging in an affair with this curvy little angel. One who's got a devilish side under the innocent facade.

No fucking way.

A firm lecture clogs in my throat, words I'd scold Micah with directed at myself and this ridiculous urge to take Nora up on her offer. Because who knows how she'll feel in another hour or two? Once she's settled, the adrenaline faded from her system, maybe she'll come to her senses and realize she doesn't want me after all—a thick, grizzly bear of a man.

"Interest isn't the issue," I admit, gritting through clenched teeth. "Your current condition is. Maybe you're usually this spontaneous and reckless or maybe you're underestimating the impact a quick tumble down the side of a mountain can do to your head."

"You're determined to remain a gentleman, aren't you?" She huffs in exasperation, an adorable pout forming on her mouth. A mouth still red and swollen from my kiss, and I have to tamp down a possessive growl—the pervasive need to claim those lips again.

Not the time.

No one's ever accused me of being a gentleman before. Goes to show how little she knows me.

"How about we compromise?" She shuffles backward and eases onto the edge of the bed. Tully rounds the mattress to rest his head on her knees, begging for pets, which Nora happily gives. The slow caress along his head and flank is mesmerizing; I imagine the gentle touch smoothing over my own tightly wound muscles, soothing the heavy tension that never quite leaves me.

"A compromise."

She nods enthusiastically. "The weather won't let up for a while, so we're stuck together for the foreseeable future. I'll rest more to assuage your concern, and we can revisit this conversation in a few hours. Sound like a plan?"

A reluctant bubble of amusement balloons in my gut. I have to give it to her. This woman's got a hell of a stubborn streak, and the bold determination heightens my desire to claim and tame it like a rustler chasing down a wild mustang. Except I don't want to break Nora, just bend her a little. Like over my favorite recliner. Or the dining table. Or even the hood of my truck.

"You don't give up, do you?" A grin tugs at the side of my mouth.

"Nope. Now, shoo." She playfully waves me away before climbing under the blankets, tucking herself in like a good girl. "I need peace and quiet while I recuperate." A saucy wink follows the statement, and this time, I allow the laugh stuck in my chest to escape.

"As you wish, angel."

THE CONSTANT DRONE of snowflakes rattling against the window interrupts an otherwise quiet afternoon. It's a familiar reminder of past winters spent alone—just me and Tully.

But I don't have to be alone tonight.

I have an angel in my bed—a cozy bundle of curves who wants me. A woman whose curious mix of courage and innocence is more alluring than any store-bought perfume worn by previous women intent on seduction. How am I supposed to resist? Especially when we're stuck together for at least another day until the snow melts?

You can't.

Give in.

The tempting whisper taunts me. For once, maybe I *can* be the lucky Olson brother. I may not be the golden boy like Micah, but I sure as hell can give Nora exactly what she wants and then some.

Tucked away on the mountain, rules don't apply. I can loosen the reins, stop trying to set an example, stop trying to keep others in line, and focus on spending a weekend under the covers with a sexy little redhead. Let comparisons with my brother's past reckless behavior evaporate like fog on the lake.

Entering the mudroom for more firewood, a sharp, minty fragrance tickles my nose. The stack of birch logs I split earlier in the week rests against the wall in a neat pyramid, and the orderly sight pleases me. It serves as a reminder that my life resembles those tidy knots and grooves.

Micah, Asa, and Tully form the base while Olson-Keller Lumber & Construction is the stable second-level, but nothing sits atop it all. The realization stops me in my tracks, an armful of logs held against my chest. I'm missing the point that everything else leads to—something or someone to make it all worthwhile.

For years, I've been content with what I have.

I co-own a successful company and maintain two close relationships—one with my brother and another with my best friend. I built the cabin I'm standing in and provide for my dog. But that's it.

I've been satisfied with the bare minimum, and I didn't even realize it until now.

No wonder I'm always grumpy, according to Micah.

My chest tightens as if one of the restraining belts broke at the lumberyard, sending hundreds of logs rolling down to crush me beneath their weight. Splinters of wood dig into my flexing fingertips, but the slight pain does nothing to relieve the bands around my heart.

And neither does the sight that greets me when I step into the main living area: Nora wrapped in one of my long-sleeved flannels with only one button holding the two sides together, leaving miles upon miles of luminous curves open to refuel my hunger.

Is Nora the answer to a question I hadn't even thought to ask?

The key to a future I never envisioned for myself?

CHAPTER FIVE

NORA

Sleeping came easier than I thought, though dreams of princes and winter storms swirled into a maelstrom of passionate kisses that kept me from feeling truly rested. Not that I'm complaining. Anything's better than the nightmares I had earlier about high school.

Glancing at the clock by the bedside, a mischievous grin works its way across my mouth. Rhett's required hours of rest have passed, which means we're officially able to pick up where we left off. Despite an arduous beginning to the day, my body and head feel no worse for wear, and a reluctant appreciation for Rhett's pushiness to get me to rest froths forward.

Now you're energized enough to fuck him ten ways to Sunday.

Goose pimples prick along my bare legs, and a twinge of embarrassment follows as I spot the folded pair of sweatpants Rhett offered. They'd made it halfway up my thick thighs before I gave up trying to make them fit.

Men's clothing is cut different from women's. There's nothing to be embarrassed about.

Logic cuts the brief moment of shame, and my therapist's suggestion of re-framing negative thoughts echoes in my head. *Turn it into something positive.* Catching a glimpse of my reflection in the window, I see the obvious silver lining: pants aren't needed for seduction. I pull the shirt and flannel I'm wearing closer until the exaggerated outline of my hips and ass show, and I can't resist a little wiggle to brighten my mood.

"How can he refuse this?" I joke, keeping my voice down.

Heavy footsteps sound from the other room, catapulting me into action. Stripping off the tee and throwing it on the bed, I tug the flannel back on—leaving one button strategically closed at my hips. The cloth strains across the wide expanse, but at least this shirt is over-sized enough to work for my purposes. It's not like I plan on wearing it for long, anyway.

Shaking out a sudden bout of nerves, my lungs contract around a deep breath. I'm really doing this. No fear and no regrets. Even if Rhett decides to turn me down.

He won't. He kissed you like a madman.

Floorboards groan beneath me as I leave the bedroom and head down a short hallway. The walls are bare, but it doesn't feel cold. The unique characteristics of the wood grain add rustic warmth and charm. Dim light filters inside, reaching the highest corners of a vaulted ceiling, and Tully's black head lifts from its perch on a couch arm.

"Hey, boy." I scratch behind his ears, smiling as he contorts himself into an awkward twist so I can rub his belly, too. "You're such a good boy, aren't you?"

"He knows a good thing when he sees it. Like a pretty girl giving him attention."

Anticipation zings through my gut like a flurry of volleys in the middle of a competitive tennis match. Rhett's raspy voice elicits a visceral reaction in my body—skin tingling, belly quivering—something a man's simple words have never done before.

Turning to face him fully, instant lust slams into me at the vision he makes standing arms full of chopped logs, muscles bulging against his sleeves, and it makes women's fascination with lumberjacks crystal clear. Because *hot damn,* does he look delicious.

"And do you?"

He raises a dark brow in question, and I clarify, "Do you know a good thing when you see it?" My fingers trace the lone button keeping me from being completely exposed to him, reveling in the heated gaze he darts towards the movement.

"Angel, I've no doubt you're the greatest damn thing that's landed in my life in years."

A furious blush erupts at the outrageous compliment. *Well, someone clearly had a change of heart in the past few hours.* Which bodes well for the both of us.

"In that case..." I lick my lips, searching for a sexy segue into my previous proposition as I play with the ends of my hair. When my finger gets stuck in a tangle, inspiration strikes. "Here's what's going to happen: I'm going to take a long, hot shower, and I'd prefer it if you'd join me." His facial expression remains neutral, though I swear I just heard a muted growl rumble in the room. My voice drops to a lower octave, the silky quality meant to brook no refusal, as I up the ante. "If you listen close enough, you might even hear *how much* I want you to."

With the provocative words hanging in the air, I twirl around to saunter into the master bedroom's bathroom suite—leaving Rhett with one last come-hither glance over my shoulder, praying he follows me.

You'd never know this is my first seduction, I muse. Even I'm surprised by the bold steps I've taken, my courage expanding to astronomical heights. No wonder women feel powerful when seducing a man; it carries a rush of adrenaline that makes you drunk on its effects—obliterating every previous doubt you held about yourself.

Flannel flutters to the white bathroom tile before I turn the brass knobs in the walk-in shower. Steam slowly paints the diamond pattern on the walls and wonder sets in as I lean into the sizzling stream of water.

Am I really going to follow through with this plan?

To masturbate within his hearing, hoping to lure him like a siren in the sea?

Hell yes.

Wicked smirk on my mouth, my hands cup my breasts, squeezing them together as I fantasize about overflowing Rhett's rough palms. Obviously, the man needs absolute certainty from a woman before agreeing to fuck her, which I appreciate, but damn! I don't know how many more signals I can send, when I know his reticence isn't for a lack of interest.

My nipples harden at the brush of my thumbs, and the round drops of water clinging to the plumped up globes starts a throbbing in my pussy. I picture Rhett's tongue lapping at each tantalizing drop while I offer myself to him, a deep instinct to serve and please him rising like an ocean tide.

God, where is he?

As if attuned to my inner thoughts, the bathroom door slams against the counter heralding his arrival. A satisfied taunt starts to emerge when he barges into the shower—soaking his clothes in the process—and whips me around until I'm bent over the sink, dripping water onto the floor.

"What—"

His palm snaps against my ass with a loud crack while my yelp of surprise resounds in the room. "You really thought you could touch yourself in my shower and get away with it?" Another smack. "You want this, angel? Then you're damn well gonna get it—*my way*."

Mhmm. Okay, whatever you say.

The words stall in my throat, but I force my head into a shaky nod of agreement. Hindsight twenty-twenty, I should've guessed he'd be a dominant lover once he finally committed himself. Not that the knowledge would've stopped me from pursuing him, but I might've been a little more prepared for this current situation.

"You may think you have control with all of your teasing, but you don't." He rubs a soothing circle over one butt cheek. "I'll fuck this cunt however I want whenever I want. It's all in my timing, and you're just gonna take it. Is that understood?"

This time I manage a weak affirmation before he resumes what I can only assume is my punishment for provoking him. He grunts in approval, a whispered "Good girl" tickling my shoulder, as his other hand snakes forward and dives between my parted thighs.

"This from me or the shower?" His fingertips easily dip inside me and my muscles clench reflexively, trying to keep him there.

"Need me to stroke your ego, mountain man?" A ragged breath huffs out when he adds another spanking in response. *Fuck, that's starting to burn.* The kind of heat meant to melt away pain and replace it with fiery pleasure. The kind of heat I've only ever read about in books.

"Come on, that's not what you really want to stroke, is it?" His hot breath mingles with the coolness of wet hair against my ear, and an involuntary shiver presses me closer to his firm body—the combustible combination a thunderstorm raining down on every nerve. "Look up, Nora. I wanna see those angel eyes."

Our gazes clash in the mirror above the sink—a brilliant intensity glittering in Rhett's green gaze. "Why do you call me that?" I ask stupidly, distracted by the sight. He's looking at me like I'm a five-course meal, and he hasn't eaten in days; it's an unnerving feeling. No one's ever wanted me as badly as it seems Rhett does. What if I don't live up to his fantasy?

Especially when he's blowing mine out of the water.

"Because you fucking glowed in the snow. Pure white innocence painted with gold—a mythical creature come to life." Pleasure radiates from where he circles my clit, increasing the friction, and all I can focus on is my reflection watching hungrily, my body rocking against his hand to pressure him to hurry. "But I can see you're more than that now. You're a flesh and blood woman with a taste for the wicked. Isn't that right?"

Quick, successive strikes to my ass coincide with three intertwined fingers slamming deep into my pussy, matching the harsh rhythm. My belly, love handles—*everything*—jiggle in reaction, but instead of turning Rhett off, it seems to ignite his passion as he refuses to ease the aggressive bombardment to my senses.

Pain turns to pleasure, turns to something resembling a live wire, short-circuiting my brain and drawing every muscle taut. "Rhett…" The garbled syllable gets lost under a cloak of heavy breathing and the clap of skin against skin. This is too much. I can't handle this.

"Come for me, angel. Show me how well this cunt will soak my dick." He nips the side of my neck. "And if you're a really good girl, I'll soothe this cherry red ass with my tongue before rewarding your pussy for letting me fuck you so hard."

A strangled moan bubbles over at the filthy promise, and it sends my orgasm rocketing through me in a blinding rush of euphoria. Knees turning to jelly, I collapse into Rhett's broad chest as the hand he used to spank me takes to patting my skin in calming caresses.

Unintelligible murmurs rumble at my back. Praise, judging by the tone of the fleeting slips of words pressed beneath my ear. Tilting my head to the side, I search for a closer connection—a kiss.

Shaky. Dazed.

I need Rhett's confident claim to ground me, and he doesn't disappoint.

Mouth slanting over mine—bristly beard chafing already sensitized skin—a sense of possession passes between us. An ownership that sinks deep into my bones, imprinting itself in my DNA.

Rhett's mine.

I'm his.

And the intuitive knowledge settles my chaotic thoughts, prompts me to stake my own claim on his body like he did with mine. Reaching a hand back, I run my fingers through his hair, massaging his scalp, and break away from him long enough to whisper, "I want to do something for you now."

He groans, nuzzling my cheek. "That's not necessary, sweetheart. This isn't a tit for tat."

"I know, but I want to." Spinning around in his arms, wet clothing plasters his body, molding to every inch of muscle. "Please?" I slide my naked curves along his front, rocking harder into the thick erection notched between my thighs.

"Damn, I lose all willpower when it comes to you. You make me wanna give you whatever will make you happy."

Biting my lip to disguise a smile of victory, I shrug. "It's not as if the feeling isn't mutual." My hands hasten to drag the soaked cotton of his shirt up over his head, thankful Rhett doesn't put up much resistance. "All I've been able to think about since waking in your bed is how to get you in it with me. How willing I am to do whatever you wish in order to satisfy you."

"You realize we both sound crazy, right?" he asks once his head is free of the shirt collar. And damn is he fine. Inches taller than me, thick slabs of muscle stack upon each other to form a stocky torso I'm dying to explore. Dark curls arrow downward into the perfect vee, begging me to tear away his jeans to reveal my prize.

"Call it cabin fever."

"After five hours?"

"Sudden onset." I wink before struggling with the silver button at his waist. With his help, we finally manage to strip the tough denim away until we both stand naked, the forgotten shower still sounding in the background.

I'd read books before with the big dick trope, but they never seemed like that big of a deal.

A dick is a dick as long as a man knows how to use it.

Except now I know that its a trope for a reason because Rhett's sporting the largest cock I've ever seen, and curiosity settles in my pussy because it's definitely going to stretch me to the limit.

"Is this why you were so reluctant earlier? Because of this beast?" I tentatively joke. One finger draws a line down his chest but stops short of his pelvis.

"No, I'd completely forgotten about it." He gestures below with a nonchalant wave of his hand, and a disbelieving chuckle bubbles up.

"Seriously?"

How does a man forget about the anaconda he's packing?

Do you think about your pussy all the time?

Point taken.

"It's not like I go around playing with my dick twenty-four seven. Sorry if it wasn't first to mind after saving you from certain death."

Exasperation winds its way through his body, so I decide to lay off the questions. What's it matter, anyway? He's got it, and I want it. Plain and simple.

"It's a damn shame you don't play with it more often." Wrapping my hand around what girth I can encircle, I squeeze wistfully. "But consider the position taken because we're about to become fast friends. It's gonna become my favorite pastime."

Sinking to my knees, every cell in my body aches to please him, especially after the orgasm he gave me. But instead of harsh and domineering, I want to go slow. Lazily suck on him like he's the last lollipop I'll ever have.

Then the realization hits me: he's the last *cock* I ever want to have.

Girl, you are in capital T trouble.

CHAPTER SIX

RHETT

Did I say Micah was the lucky brother? Because damn if Nora isn't proving me wrong. Her chestnut eyes sparkle with a languorous contentment as she leans forward and surrounds the tip of my cock with plump lips. The damp touch of her tongue almost brings me to my knees, and my hands slam to the counter behind her, knuckles whitening in an effort to steady myself.

When she dared me to join her in the shower earlier, I couldn't help but admire her stubborn determination—her nap clearly doing nothing but shore up more of her resolve. Her sassy strut into my bedroom, the sound of the shower starting. It all converged into an irresistible image of her naked in my arms while I proved to her who exactly was in charge here.

Vibrations from her pleased moan hum along my cock, and I swear that sound will haunt me long after she leaves me.

Don't think about it.

Don't let her go.

Micah likes to joke about me becoming a caveman when I find a woman of my own, and everything in me yearns to follow through on his prediction. Yet, a niggling fear holds me back: Nora won't be happy here. Her life requires more than a solitary existence on the mountain. No doubt her fans will tire of seeing the same trees every day.

She can drive to town, moron.

Except sometimes the roads get blocked. Sometimes the internet goes out. All manner of things occur up here and judging by her decision to brave a blizzard on her own today, Nora doesn't strike me as the wilderness type. She might be able to handle a fling on the weekend, but nothing long-term that keeps her away from the creature comforts of town and the entertainment to be had there.

"Why do I get the feeling you're not with me anymore?" Nora leans back on her heels, her swollen lips pouting in a disappointed moue. And I'm the dumbest fuck this side of the mountain to be distracted by an unknown future when the woman of my dreams is literally kneeling before me.

"If I'm doing something wrong or you don't like..."

"No, you're perfect." I glance down at my wilting erection and embarrassment swallows me whole. "I... I just can't seem to get my mind to turn off." An issue I've had a couple of times before when my thoughts got the best of me, but for it to happen with Nora is the nail in the coffin. Stuffing my dick back in my jeans, I shuffle away—needing distance, a breather.

Water pouring down the shower drain drones in the background, giving me a brief reprieve as I turn it off. The sudden absence of noise is jarring and stresses what just happened between us.

Me spanking her juicy ass until she came on my hand.

Her sucking my dick until I let worry and fear ruin the moment.

Some man in charge I am. The minute I'm not pleasing her, my mind jumps into worry mode.

"I understand. My brain tends to over-think, too, and it can be difficult to shut down." Pushing to her feet, Nora hurries to grab a dry towel hanging from a hook in the wall, quickly wrapping it around her body. "Do you mind if I ask what you were thinking about?"

I scratch the back of my neck, shame still running rampant through my body. "You. Me. What we're doing." Starting to feel suffocated in the small space, I slide by her to get to the bedroom before heading towards the open living area.

How the hell did Asa do this with Poppy?

The most standoffish of our trio—even called the Beast by some of the idiot townspeople because of his looks and attitude—he'd somehow managed to find and keep his woman within a weekend. Didn't let fear of the future, of her leaving, stop him from taking what he wanted.

Didn't let it affect the parts of his anatomy needed to express exactly how much he wanted her either.

"Hey, I'm sorry if I pushed too hard." Nora follows me a few minutes later, changed into my clothes again, only this time her intention is obviously to show as little skin as possible versus her ensemble earlier. And again, I curse my stupidity. "All I thought about was myself: being spontaneous, voicing my desires despite any fears, and I didn't really listen to your refusals—just kinda went with the surface level physical attraction I saw from you. I'm so sorry if I made you uncomfortable."

"You don't need to apologize; you weren't alone in this. I did—*I do* want you, *badly*. Your ass probably still bears the evidence of how much I want you, but what's going to happen once the snow melts?" White flakes continue to ping against the cabin, indicating more hours stuck together, but eventually it will stop. Which means Nora will leave. And my head won't let me ignore that looming event, won't let me enjoy even a fucking night with her—no matter how hard I try to rationalize and urge myself to be happy in the moment.

Why torture myself by knowing what I'll lose after her departure? It'll be hard enough knowing the heat of her cunt around my fingers, the soft roundness of her ass against my palm, the fucking heaven of her mouth.

I don't need to add another chain linking me to her.

I've forged enough to last a lifetime.

CHAPTER SEVEN

NORA

"**I** 'll be here with you and Tully." The German Shepherd remains in his spot on the couch, watching our conversation from the sidelines.

"Not for long," he mutters, pacing in front of the window, every now and then glaring outside like he finds the weather offensive. *Mercurial man.* Dominant, stubborn, *confusing*. Rhett's reaction in the bathroom had knocked me down a few pegs.

I know real men aren't like the ones in fiction, but it dented my confidence feeling his cock lose some of its steel in my mouth. Weren't men supposed to love blowjobs? Supposed to be wild for them?

The two times I'd done it before, I found my head being forced further and further down without a care in the world for my comfort, yet Rhett never reached such a level of need. And while I understand the power of distracting thoughts, my ego's still taking a hit.

"Soon you'll return home to your thousands of followers. I thought I'd be okay with a quick fling. Hell, my brother did it all the time. I figured I could, too." A self-deprecating laugh grates through the air, the harsh judgment of himself summoning a wealth of empathy. I know what it's like to want something and finding yourself unable to attain it. To slog through a pit of quicksand desperate to suck you under, determination weighing heavily on your shoulders as you get no closer to your goal. "But I can't do that with you."

"Because you're afraid I'll leave." It's a statement, not a question.

"Because you don't belong here, and if we fuck... If I touch you anymore..." He spits out unfinished sentences, muscles bunching along his shoulders, throat working to explain. "Suffice it to say, I'm saving us from having to learn the hard way that it won't work."

"The hard way," I repeat, skeptical. "Which would be us breaking up because I can't stand the solitude here with you?" It's a stretch, but the hazarded guess seems to hit its mark as Rhett jerks his chin in agreement.

Stupid boy.

Endearing man.

We've barely known each other a day, and he's already thinking so far ahead that he's planning on how to protect us from heartbreak before it's even a possibility. And I thought *I* over-analyzed too much; my therapist would have a field day with Rhett.

"Mountain living is hard," Rhett adds, oblivious to the exasperation etching itself on my face. "It's not like a fairy tale. We lose power. We get snowed in." He gestures out the window where a wall of snow covers half of the glass pane. "And your precious internet won't always be available. No streaming live for your fans. What will you do then?"

The look in his eyes and the tension around his mouth make my heart skip a beat. I recognize that fear. The worry that you're not good enough. It's something that's played in my head for my whole life when it comes to my weight, and here's Rhett feeling the same way.

Determined to break through his wall, I ignore his prediction, shrugging my shoulders. "You realize I live in High Ridge, right? The little mountain town twenty minutes away? A town that houses your successful company? I can work from anywhere, even in this cabin secluded from town. If you're able to make it work, so can I."

He shakes his head in denial. "You're so god-damned stubborn."

"You know you like it. Lets your inner Neanderthal come out to play in an attempt to temper me." I'd hoped the teasing would lighten the strain in the air, but no luck.

"I'm not joking, Nora."

The use of my name and not his usual *angel* comes as a shock, and it ushers in another unfortunate emotion: resignation. Rhett isn't prepared to compromise or budge, and I have no control over this outcome.

I can argue until I'm blue in the face, praying he finally trusts me enough to give this a shot—whatever *this* is—but it won't matter until Rhett's ready to decide for himself what risk he's willing to take.

Slumping into an armchair, Tully must sense my melancholy because he whines before trotting over to me, resting his head in my lap. "I know you aren't, which is why I'm done trying to convince you to give us a chance." The abrupt one-eighty stops him in his tracks.

Silky fur runs between my fingers as I stroke the spot between Tully's ears, battling the sudden urge to cry. "You think you're doing what's best, while I don't agree. We've got a connection, however instantaneous it was, but I deserve more than a man unwilling to even meet me halfway to explore it. Maybe in the past I would've accepted half-measures, but not anymore. I've worked too hard on myself to backslide."

Even if it means losing the first man I've ever had such a wild attraction to.

The first man I felt an instant connection with.

CHAPTER EIGHT

RHETT

You're a fucking coward.

Shame slithers to the bottom of my gut, curling its scaly length into a tight immovable ball. Nora has been vulnerable and brave all day. Hell, she started her day that way by hiking into a blizzard. Yet I've kept myself closed off in an effort to be responsible, allowing the glimpse of an epiphany to crack my shell for an instant, before I snapped shut and reverted to good ole reliable Rhett Olson.

The man who criticized his brother for claiming a woman after one night.

The man who scolded his best friend for being unable to keep his hands off his woman at the lumberyard.

The man who's got a stick so far up his ass trying to overcome a history full of youthful transgressions that he's alienated his hometown even more and kept his family and friends at an arm's length, always holding himself to a so-called *higher standard* in order to look after them, protect them.

When they're grown men who have families of their own and don't need his particular brand of caring—or rather, *control*.

Fuck me, I've been a real asshole.

"You're right, and I apologize for being such a—" The room goes pitch black as the electricity cuts off, the gentle hum of appliances disappearing in a blink. "Shit. That's what I was afraid of happening; we've lost power."

"But you're used to this, right?" Surprisingly, I don't hear fear in her voice, only trust that I'll see us through the storm safely, and the coil of shame winds tighter.

"Yeah, Tully and I usually hole up in the bedroom with a fire going, but there's enough wood stacked in the mudroom for me to keep two fires lit, so we're not stuck sharing a bed."

"We were moments away from sharing one for an entirely different reason fifteen minutes ago." She chuckles good-naturedly at the reminder. "So, I think we can handle the necessity of sharing a room together to conserve resources. It'll almost be like camping, except we have a comfy bed and fluffy blankets."

Grateful that my harsh mood earlier hasn't completely dampened her spirits, a slight smile forges forward. "Alright, I guess we're camping in my room, then. Extra blankets are in the closet over there." I point to a closed door in the hallway. "And I'll grab some snacks."

An excited squeal bursts from Nora as she jumps to her feet, Tully mirroring her enthusiasm with a swift woof and happy swish of his tail. "I realize things are serious, but my parents never let me sleepover at friends' houses. This is kind of a childhood dream fulfilled."

"Except for the part where a gaggle of girls talk about boys and makeup and whatever other topics fascinate twelve-year-olds."

"Stereotype much?" Nora raises an expressive eyebrow and smirks. "Besides, who wants to talk about boys when you're spending the night with a man? Scandalous!" This time, both brows wiggle in an over-blown expression of shock, and a bark of laughter doubles me over.

"Opposed to your scandalous seduction of said man?" I tease, appreciating the light banter. Nora's laughter brightens the room, tumbling behind her retreating form as she heads towards the closet for those blankets, and while I'm glad we're back on neutral ground, the détente surely won't last long once we're forced into closer proximity in my room.

The sparks between us are on a simmer, taking a backseat due to the power outage, but it won't take much to flame back into a raging fire.

AFTER A COMFORTABLE dinner and multiple rounds of an old word game Nora found deep in the closet, we settle on opposite sides of my bed with the fire at our feet—fully clothed in my pajamas, a marked difference from how we started our day. "What convinced you to start living your life so..." *Carefree. Fear-defying.* I struggle to voice my curiosity.

"Spontaneously? Too brazenly?" She jokes from her place on my left, rolling to her side to face me, firelight casting dancing shadows across her cheeks.

"Your words, not mine." *But yes, exactly.*

"It's a long story." Her nails pick at a loose thread on the comforter blanketing us. "My weight's always been a struggle, though it didn't bother me until I hit puberty. That's when I got rounder. *All over.*" She glances up at me, eyes widened for emphasis, like it was the worst thing ever.

"Everyone noticed, and they all commented from my mother to the bullies at school. It became so bad that I was afraid to do much of anything for fear of drawing attention to myself. Eventually, I started therapy, which has helped me grow in confidence and self-worth, but it's not like I'm completely cured. While unconscious today, I dreamed of past trauma. And today's been a lesson in learning how to find the balance between my healthy and unhealthy fear."

I digest her words, their impact like a meteor slamming me to Earth. Righteous anger. Intense admiration. Riotous emotions trampling any preconceived notions I had of her.

Swallowing past the lump lodged in my throat, I ask, "Is this what you discuss with your followers?"

"What? Why?"

"Because I can see why they'd love you. You're strong and courageous despite people hurting you. You decided to change your life for the better when you could've wallowed in the pain—let it drown you." And the truth is blinding: she's braver than I am. I walk and talk like I've got everything figured out, like I'm in control, but I'm still allowing the past to define me.

Hell, I wouldn't even give myself a night with this beautiful, spirited woman because of a whole host of imagined reasons.

Flopping back to stare at the wooden-beamed ceiling, Nora sighs. "I like your perspective, even if most of the time it doesn't feel like such a big deal to me. Lots of people have issues and deal with them; it doesn't really make me special or anything."

"You couldn't be more wrong." Deciding it's time to take a page out of her book, I continue, "You already know I have a younger brother, and in our family, I've always been the one to look out for him. Growing up on the wrong side of town, judged by people because of it, I can't admit to being a choirboy, but I grew out of my wild phase. Micah never did until he met Kate."

What a godsend she'd turned out to be.

"Somewhere along the line, I elevated myself to the role of parent for Micah and Asa long past the time it was needed. Scolding them for so-called bad decisions. And holding myself at a distance to fit the reformed mold I tried to fit them in. Out of fear of being seen as... Hypocritical? Irresponsible? No better than the troubled family I came from? I don't know."

It's a relief to voice what's been pummeling my heart and head today. To be free with my emotions and fears. No wonder Nora's so insistent on living this way: it provides a pressure release for all the pent-up thoughts and feelings.

Something I'm beginning to understand I've needed for years now.

CHAPTER NINE

NORA

That explains his hesitancy over jumping headfirst into a fling or a relationship with me. Appreciating his honesty, an unexpected and inappropriate giggle bubbles up.

"Sorry, I'm not laughing at you. It's just that we've done this all backwards. We should've chatted, gotten to know each other first, then kissed then, well, you know." Our interlude in the bathroom seems so long ago—almost like a dream—and I can only blame myself for wanting to rush into things.

"Do you regret letting me touch you?" Gentle concern emanates from Rhett, his handsome face coming into view as he leans over to gauge my reaction.

Turning the tables, I ask, "Do you regret touching me?"

"No. Those stolen moments are unforgettable. You're etched into my soul—the beautiful angel I found on the mountain."

His head drops lower until our breaths mingle in the sliver of space separating us. A quiver of anxiety shadows reawakened desire. "Please don't if you're not ready, if you're unsure." *Another rejection would be too much.* "I'm not asking for forever, but a willingness to explore without recriminations—without holding yourself back."

Rhett sighs. "And that's what you deserve..." He remains quiet. Considering. Deciding. Until he finally relinquishes control. Chooses to trust me. "Alright, I'll follow your lead in this adventure together, but know that I'm in charge in the bedroom."

Sugary delight makes my teeth ache at how sweet it is to hear Rhett's commitment to fight for our relationship. And I won't let him regret it.

"I never thought otherwise, considering your actions earlier."

"Good." He flips to his back and motions me forward. "Now, I need you soft and ready, angel. Open for my cock, eager for my possession. Put your pussy flush against my mouth."

Oh, hell... I've never ridden a man's face before, and jokes aside, I really could hurt him with my weight. I want to follow his instructions. But I'm scared.

And the irony is not lost on me.

Damn, another insecurity flare-up.

This is logic, not insecurity.

My eyes study Rhett, prone on his back, sturdy like a deep-rooted tree, but still, even trees can be felled. And I could be the wrecking ball. *You're mixing your metaphors.*

"Nora? What's wrong?"

"I don't want to hurt you."

"You won't."

"That's the gentlemanly thing to say, but reality says different." *Along with the boys from school.*

"I've never been accused of being a gentleman, and I'm not gonna start now. Get your ass up here and sit on my face before I decide to increase your spankings for defying me this long." His palm twitches like it's preparing to make good on his threat, and an indecent moan escapes my lips before I can stop it.

"You're gonna spank me?" *Is that my breathy voice?*

"Don't pretend you didn't enjoy it earlier." The man has the nerve to smirk. "Of course I'm gonna palm your juicy ass while I eat this cunt. Now, come here."

Yes, sir.

I kick off the underwear I put on since none of Rhett's sweats fit me, and I shuffle to my knees, straddling his waist, uncomfortable going straight to straddling his face. But he doesn't let me get away with the move, confident hands dragging my hips forward until I hover over his mouth, his hot breath grazing my inner thighs.

"Sweetheart, you're not going to hurt me; trust me." The words whisper through my curls before Rhett forces me down, anchoring me against his mouth.

A surprised "oh" flutters in the air at the novel sensation—slick presses of his tongue, hungry suckles of his lips. Lashes drifting lower, my eyes close as my head tilts back, hands gripping the headboard for stability as I rock into Rhett's mouth.

Humming groans of pleasure vibrate from below, and I can't help driving harder into the sensation, concern for Rhett flying out the window as his fingers dig deeper into my hips to pull me closer instead of pushing me away—one hand fulfilling his promise as it firmly swats my ass.

Slick glides of my body against his fill the room, and firelight warms my back as indecent shadows are cast along the walls.

The curve of my breasts swaying with each press into Rhett's mouth.

Arms bending to the headboard.

Rhett's cock tenting the blanket.

Reaching back, I smooth my hand under the covers and the elastic of a waistband until my fingers curl around him. Pre-cum coats my thumb as I swipe it over the head, causing Rhett to jerk.

"Angel, what the hell do you think you're doing?" The words are muffled, but I understand them well enough.

"I didn't want you feeling left out." Another caress of my thumb draws a hiss before I begin pumping him in earnest. As if I dropped the yellow flag, a race to the finish erupts. Rhett thrusting his tongue deep then focusing on my clit in rhythmic sucks. Me squeezing the enormous pole in my hand, intermittently stroking the twin balls beneath.

Too soon, our movements become erratic. The sensations too much.

Everything centers on my clit, every nerve exploding in pleasure as my climax hits—something closely followed by Rhett's hoarse shout and his thick essence seeping through my fingers.

Forehead resting against the headboard, my lungs gasp for air, while Rhett brushes light kisses over every exposed part of me he can reach—overly sensitized clit, clenching core, inner thighs.

When a semblance of calm settles in my bones, I inch back, falling to my side next to him. Though, he doesn't allow me much space before dragging one leg over his hip and lining up his still hard cock to my pussy. "Ready for more, angel?"

All I can achieve is a slight dip of my chin—amazed by his stamina—but it's all the affirmation he needs before easing inside, the thick intrusion stretching me to the limit.

Big dick, indeed.

CHAPTER TEN

RHETT

Nora's heat engulfs me as I slowly sink into her wet pussy, and I lick away that same wetness from my lips, enjoying the leftover taste from her riding my tongue. Like a true angel, she's all sweet sugar and pure light—a white-hot glow that incinerates every doubt and fear I held.

Because something this good can't be wrong.

I'm choosing to imitate Micah and Asa for once. Choosing to keep my woman and hold on to her for dear life—scorning any pestering negative thoughts that want me to doubt my decision. It's time I stopped living the half-life of a grumpy hermit. And I've even got an angel to help me.

Glancing down, a growl of appreciation forms at the sight of her pretty pink opening accepting me, my dick gleaming with her cream, and plunging deeper for more. "Do you know how sexy you look, sucking me in like the good little angel girl you are? So fucking gorgeous."

I watch her throat work to swallow before she answers in a husky whisper. "Probably about as sexy as you look all bearded and flannel-y."

Yeah, these pajamas need to go real soon, but I refuse to waste time with clothing removal while her pussy is wrapped around my dick.

"Impossible." I grunt, though I appreciate how attractive she finds me. It boosts my ego even if it's unnecessary.

"Don't underestimate your—" She breaks off with a sharp inhale as I bury the last few inches of my cock in a swift thrust.

"You were saying?" I taunt with a swivel of my hips, methodically increasing the speed of my strokes until Nora's eyes glaze over, like dark chocolate melting over a strawberry, a flush rising high on the apple of her cheeks.

Sweat dampens my grip on her leg as I shift my forearm under her knee to lift her body to a different angle as I work to hit that special spot inside her on every plunge.

"Stop... trying... to make me... talk." Each labored word huffs out in exasperation, and I chuckle at the adorable frustration emanating from my angel. Her hand reaches down to hurry things along, but I catch it with a disapproving tsking sound.

"Uh uh. I'm in charge, remember?" To prove my point, I force myself to pause—gritting my teeth to ignore the encouraging pulsing of her pussy—and lean forward to nip a rosy nipple. "It's my pace or nothing at all. Got it?"

Her nails dig into my shoulders in retribution for the quick bite, but she quickly nods, and I resume the previous pace, though I can't resist suckling the swollen buds before me, drowning in the sweet scent between her breasts that is uniquely Nora.

Seconds.

Minutes.

Hours could've passed without our knowledge, too engrossed in each other to notice something as ordinary as time. Even the lighting remains unchanged despite the later hour, due to the pile of white snow reflecting through the window.

"Please, Rhett... I can't take much more," Nora's plea pierces the sensual haze clouding my mind. A part of me doesn't want this to end—wants to prolong this moment for as long as possible, our first time together—but I don't want her to become too sore.

The night is long, and we're free to explore it without risk of the outside world intruding.

Giving in, my fingers circle her clit as I pound into her with harsh thrusts until she finally tips over the edge, tugging me with her—both of us groaning in pleasure.

This is what I needed.

Our breaths caress each other's skin in the cooling air.

Our hearts stammer out matching beats.

And the walls I'd built around myself lay forever decimated at her feet.

EPILOGUE ONE

NORA
ONE YEAR LATER

"What's it like having your very own lumberjack?"

Tons of hearts cover the screen of my live video, and I laugh at everyone's enthusiasm. My followers love when I mention Rhett. They can't get enough of him, and neither can I.

Panning the camera towards my man as he directs a group of men bringing in a load of timber, I zoom in on his muscular body, covered in worn plaid and jeans. His style hasn't varied in all the time we've been together, but I don't care because he looks damn good in the basics.

"Better than you can imagine. Scout's honor." I hold up my right hand in the facsimile of a vow. "Every night we..."

"You're not sharing our personal secrets with the world again, are you, angel?" Rhett catches my spying, and I quickly sign off with a hasty farewell. I try to respect his privacy, but is it so wrong of me to want to show him off?

He's my dream man, and I still get butterflies when I remember he's all mine.

"What? Never!"

"Good." His voice lowers as he nears. "Otherwise, I'd have to punish you, and I'd much rather reward you."

"Thankfully, those usually resemble each other in the end."

"Cheeky." I bend to avoid the swat to my ass, but he lands it anyway, before scooping me up and carrying me inside the large building central to the lumberyard. Catcalls follow us, the loudest coming from Micah and Asa, as Rhett marches by their desks until we're alone in his office.

Setting me down gently, he murmurs, "You know, I used to be a respectable business owner. I was the one catching the boys slacking off with their women, and now you're to blame for their harassment. I should spank you just for that."

Propping my elbows on the edge of his desk, I swivel my ass in his direction, daring him to fulfill the promise.

"Jesus, Nora!" The blinds slam closed so the rest of the employees can't see us anymore, and I chuckle in pleasure. *Score one point for me.* "Every day you're getting more brazen, angel."

"Thanks to you." Rhett's love and constant affirmation pairs well with my therapy sessions it turns out, and I'm feeling better than ever: mentally and emotionally. He's even joined me in a couple of sessions, allowing us to talk through some of the issues we've dealt with.

I admire the strength he's shown and his willingness to grow, especially after our unusual first meeting. Since he committed to us, it's been full steam ahead with love and devotion... and scorching hot sex. A blush blooms along my neck and cheeks as my body drops lower to entice Rhett.

My loner mountain man was hard up for some loving.

And so was I, if I'm honest.

"The fuck?" A near shout reverberates against the walls, and I wince. He discovered my secret. "You let me carry you through the office while you're not wearing underwear? Angel, you've just sealed your fate."

When the first slap of his hand strikes my ass, I whimper.

When the second hits, I moan.

And by the time he's bent behind me with his tongue burrowing between the soaked folds of my pussy, I sigh in satisfaction.

Because, in the end, this curvy girl got her man.

EPILOGUE TWO

RHETT
TWO YEARS LATER

"**D**o we have everything?" I ask, testing the strength of the bungee cord strapping everyone's furniture to the trailer hooked to my truck. Nora got together with Poppy and Kate, planning a beach vacation with our three families, a feat only the three of them thought was a good idea.

"Yep, we're all set."

"What's the matter, brother? Regretting your decision to haul all of our stuff?" Micah saunters over with my niece ensconced in his arms, her tiny arms wrapped around her father's neck.

"Hardly. I've got towing duty while you and Kate are in charge of the kids. How did Poppy and Asa manage that, anyway?"

"Because my girl's pregnant and needs peace and quiet on the road." Asa answers for him. "Plus, Micah owes us for babysitting McKayla last Friday for his date night."

"Don't act like you didn't love every minute."

Asa and Micah continue their bickering, and I grin at the welcome sight. Our lives have changed so much in the past few years with marriages and babies. Even the people of High Ridge have noticed and started treating us better—going so far as to quit using The Beast moniker for Asa.

Who knew the influence of our women would have such a radical effect?

Nora hugs me from behind, before sidling underneath my arm. "When you guys are done, we're all ready to go. The beach is calling my name!"

"And mine," Kate agrees, grabbing her squirming toddler from Micah. "Only six hours on the road is between me and dipping my toes in the ocean."

"And..." Micah dips his head to whisper something in his wife's ear that makes her blush. Shaking my head at the obvious display of affection, I turn to my own woman and grin.

"What's on the agenda for you, angel? A mermaid photo shoot? Because I'm down for a little ocean fantasy."

She laughs, the tinkling sound warming my heart. "Of course you are. But you're going to have to wait to find out what I have planned, mountain man... Or should I say, Aquaman." Her brows wriggle suggestively, and I know we're in for a good time.

My sweet angel girl is nothing if not creative. And with me by her side to make sure she's safe, she's free to be as spontaneous as she wants.

Yeah, this Olson brother definitely has some luck, after all.

Need another lonely mountain man to find love with the curvy girl of his dreams?

Check out Wood Lessons!

Anna needs a change. Her routine's become a cycle of work and home—a true hermit's lifestyle. But with a new move and job, she's ready to build the dream life she's always wanted which starts with having a home perfect for hosting friends. The first step? Commission a custom piece of furniture that leads to a fated meeting with the handsome carpenter.

Peter enjoys working with his hands. Woodworking has always been a calm escape for him until loneliness threatens his peace. But how's he supposed to find a woman holed up in his shop? Perhaps fate will have her find him because the curvy Anna looks to be just what he needs to warm up his empty bed.

When Peter offers to teach Anna "wood lessons", the match is struck for a steamy union!

A hot man in plaid meets the curvy girl of his dreams for an instalove so sweet, it's sure to make your teeth ache. Watch these two lonely people discover a love and passion that'll leave you sweating!

THANKS FOR READING & DON'T FORGET TO RATE/ REVIEW!

Please consider leaving a rating/review on Amazon, Goodreads, Instagram, TikTok, and/or any other sites you review on. Ratings & reviews are the #1 way to support an indie author like me.

They don't have to be long or even positive (though I hope you enjoyed this book!). All the algorithms care about are QUANTITY.

The more reviews, the more my books are shown to other potential readers!

And they serve as guides to readers on whether or not to take a chance on an indie author.

I appreciate your support!

XO, Hallie

ABOUT THE AUTHOR

Hallie prefers steamy, insta-love stories where curvy girls are claimed by filthy-talking heroes. And when she ran out of reading material, she decided to write her own stories. If you want a quick, hot read, she's your girl!